KU-246-199

SERIOUSLY FUNNY
the Endlessly Quotable

TERRY PRATCHETT

Doubleday

LONDON · NEW YORK · TORONTO · SYDNEY · AUCKLAND

TRANSWORLD PUBLISHERS
61–63 Uxbridge Road, London W5 5SA
www.transworldbooks.co.uk

Transworld is part of the Penguin Random House group of companies
whose addresses can be found at global.pcnguinrandomhouse.com

Penguin
Random House
UK

First published in Great Britain in 2016 by Doubleday
an imprint of Transworld Publishers

A CIP catalogue record for this book
is available from the British Library.

ISBN 9780857524300

Typeset in 13/15 pt Minion Pro by Thomson Digital Pvt Ltd, Noida, Delhi
Printed and bound by Clays Ltd, Bungay, Suffolk

Penguin Random House is committed to a sustainable
future for our business, our readers and our planet. This book
is made from Forest Stewardship Council® certified paper.

MIX
Paper from
responsible sources
FSC® C018179
www.fsc.org

1 3 5 7 9 10 8 6 4 2

C 29 0000 0743 406

CONTENTS

For the whole of my life since I was nine years old I have enjoyed words…

Words turn us from monkeys into men. We make them, change them, trace them around, eat them and live by them – they are work-horses, carrying any burden, and their usage is the skill of the author's trade, hugely versatile; there are times when the wrong word is the right word, and times when words can be manipulated so that silence shouts. Their care, feeding and indeed breeding is part of the craft of which I am a journeyman.

Terry Pratchett, Trinity College Dublin, 2010

TERRY PRATCHETT

Terry Pratchett was, and remains, among the bestselling and most quoted authors in the UK, and worldwide. He became universally known as the acclaimed creator of the global bestselling Discworld series, the first of which, *The Colour of Magic*, was published in 1983, and as an outspoken campaigner for causes ranging from animal welfare to Alzheimer's research. In all, he was the author of over fifty bestselling books, which have been translated into thirty-eight languages. His novels have been widely adapted for stage and screen, and he was the winner of multiple prizes, including the Carnegie Medal, as well as being awarded a knighthood for services to literature – though he maintained that his greatest service to literature was to avoid writing any. Having left school without A-levels, he accumulated ten honorary doctorates over his lifetime. He died in March 2015.

HUMAN
NATURE

Most of the great triumphs and tragedies of history are caused, not by people being fundamentally good or fundamentally bad, but by people being fundamentally people.

⊷ Good Omens ⊶

Real stupidity beats artificial intelligence every time.

≒ Hogfather ≒

Some humans would do anything to see if it was possible to do it. If you put a large switch in some cave somewhere, with a sign on it saying 'End-of-the-World Switch. PLEASE DO NOT TOUCH,' the paint wouldn't even have time to dry.

Thief of Time

If there was anything that depressed him more than his own cynicism, it was that quite often it still wasn't as cynical as real life.

⊷ *Guards! Guards!* ⊶

The intelligence of that creature known as a crowd is the square root of the number of people in it.

⊷ Jingo ⊶

Evil begins when you begin to treat people as
Things.

⊷ I Shall Wear Midnight ⊶

It was so much easier to blame it on Them. It was bleakly depressing to think that They were Us. If it was Them, then nothing was anyone's fault. If it was us, what did that make Me? After all, I'm one of Us. I must be. I've certainly never thought of myself as one of Them. *No one* ever thinks of themselves as one of Them. We're always one of Us. It's Them that do the bad things.

 Jingo

Sometimes I really think people ought to have to pass a *proper* exam before they're allowed to be parents. Not just the practical, I mean.

≈ *Thief of Time* ≈

Always remember that the crowd that applauds your coronation is the same crowd that will applaud your beheading. People like a show.

Going Postal

Personal's not the same as important. People just think it is.

⇌ Lords and Ladies ⇌

The phrase 'Someone ought to do something' was not, by itself, a helpful one. People who used it *never* added the rider 'and that someone is me.'

Hogfather

You take a bunch of people who don't seem any different from you and me, but when you add them all together you get this sort of huge raving maniac with national borders and an anthem.

⊱ *Monstrous Regiment* ⊰

When you seek advice from someone it's certainly not because you want them to give it. You just want them to be there while you talk to yourself.

+⟫ *Jingo* ⟪+

ROMANCE

A marriage is always made up of two people who are prepared to swear that only the *other* one snores.

The Fifth Elephant

Just erotic. Nothing kinky. It's the difference between using a feather and using a chicken.

Eric

'The female mind is certainly a devious one, my lord.'

Vetinari looked at his secretary in surprise. 'Well, of course it is. It has to deal with the male one.'

Unseen Academicals

He'd noticed that sex bore some resemblance to cookery: it fascinated people, they sometimes bought books full of complicated recipes and interesting pictures, and sometimes when they were really hungry they created vast banquets in their imagination – but at the end of the day they'd settle quite happily for egg and chips. If it was well done and maybe had a slice of tomato.

＊＝ *The Fifth Elephant* ＝＊

Hate is a force of attraction. Hate is just love with its back turned.

⊶ Maskerade ⊷

Ninety per cent of true love is acute, ear-burning embarrassment.

Wyrd Sisters

The people of Lancre thought that marriage was a very serious step that ought to be done properly, so they practised quite a lot.

⊱ *Maskerade* ⊰

LEARNING & WISDOM

Education was a bit like a communicable sexual disease. It made you unsuitable for a lot of jobs and then you had the urge to pass it on.

⇥ *Hogfather* ⇤

The truth may be out there, but lies are inside your head.

→ *Hogfather* ←

They say a little knowledge is a dangerous thing, but it is not one half so bad as a lot of ignorance.

⊨ Equal Rites ⊨

I didn't go to university. Didn't even finish
A-levels. But I have sympathy for those who
did.

⊨ alt.fan.pratchett ⊨

I'll be more enthusiastic about encouraging thinking outside the box when there's evidence of any thinking going on inside it.

⊰⊱ alt.fan.pratchett ⊰⊱

The presence of those seeking the truth is infinitely to be preferred to those who think they've found it.

Monstrous Regiment

It's still magic even if you know how it's done.

The Wee Free Men

The trouble with having an open mind, of course, is that people will insist on coming along and trying to put things in it.

⊹⊱ Diggers ⊰⊹

A European says: I can't understand this, what's wrong with me? An American says: I can't understand this, what's wrong with him?

I make no suggestion that one side or other is right, but observation over many years leads me to believe it is true.

⊹⊱ *alt.fan.pratchett* ⊰⊹

Of course, it is very important to be sober when you take an exam. Many worthwhile careers in the street-cleansing, fruit-picking and subway-guitar-playing industries have been founded on a lack of understanding of this simple fact.

≈ Moving Pictures ≈

A lie can run round the world before the truth
has got its boots on.

+≡─ *The Truth* ─≡+

The truth isn't easily pinned to a page. In the bathtub of history the truth is harder to hold than the soap and much more difficult to find.

⊸⊷ *Sourcery* ⊶⊱

I have no use for people who have learned the limits of the possible.

The Last Hero

'But we're a university! We *have* to have a library!' said Ridcully. 'It adds *tone*. What sort of people would we be if we didn't go into the library?'

'Students,' said the Senior Wrangler morosely.

⊷ *The Last Continent* ⊶

That was always the dream, wasn't it? 'I wish I'd known then what I know now'? But when you got older you found out that you *now* wasn't *you* then. You then was a twerp. You then was what you had to be to start out on the rocky road of becoming you now, and one of the rocky patches on that road was being a twerp.

≈ *Night Watch* ≈

I reckon responsible behaviour is something to get when you grow older. Like varicose veins.

≁ *Wyrd Sisters* ≁

She had heard it said that, before you could understand anybody, you needed to walk a mile in their shoes, which did not make a whole lot of sense because probably *after* you had walked a mile in their shoes you would understand that they were chasing you and accusing you of the theft of a pair of shoes – although, of course, you could probably outrun them owing to their lack of footwear.

I Shall Wear Midnight

SUCCESS

It is well known that a vital ingredient of success is not knowing that what you're attempting can't be done.

⊷ Equal Rites ⊶

There are those who, when presented with a glass that is exactly half full, say: this glass is half full.

And then there are those who say: this glass is half empty.

The world *belongs*, however, to those who can look at the glass and say: What's up with this glass? Excuse me? Excuse *me*? *This* is my glass? I don't *think* so. *My* glass was full! *And* it was a bigger glass!

+⇒ *The Truth* ⇐+

If you trust in yourself, and believe in your dreams, and follow your star… you'll still get beaten by people who spent their time working hard and learning things and weren't so lazy.

⊷ *The Wee Free Men* ⊶

The worst thing you can do is nothing.

~ *Snuff* ~

See a pin and pick it up, and all day long you'll
have a pin.

⊷ Going Postal ⊷

Vimes had got around to a Clean Desk policy. It was a Clean Floor strategy that eluded him at the moment.

⊹⊨ Thud! ⊨⊹

Destiny *is* important, see, but people go wrong when they think it controls them. It's the other way around.

⊱ *Wyrd Sisters* ⊰

If failure had no penalty success would not be a prize.

Sourcery

Give a man a fire and he's warm for a day, but set fire to him and he's warm for the rest of his life.

⊰⊱ *Jingo* ⊰⊱

Sometimes glass glitters more than diamonds
because it has more to prove.

↔ *The Truth* ↔

Only in our dreams are we free. The rest of the time we need wages.

↦ *Wyrd Sisters* ↤

Sometimes it's better to light a flamethrower than curse the darkness.

⊨ Men at Arms ⊨

LIFE & DEATH

The whole of life is just like watching a click[*], he thought. Only it's as though you always get in ten minutes after the big picture has started, and no-one will tell you the plot, so you have to work it all out yourself from the clues.

⊷ *Moving Pictures* ⊶

[*] Or in non-Discworld terms a film

Time is a drug. Too much of it kills you.

⊢⇒ Small Gods ⇐⊣

People don't alter history any more than birds
alter the sky, they just make brief patterns in it.

Mort

His philosophy was a mixture of three famous schools – the Cynics, the Stoics and the Epicureans – and summed up all three of them in his famous phrase, 'You can't trust any bugger further than you can throw him, and there's nothing you can do about it, so let's have a drink.'

— *Small Gods* —

It is important to know *when not to let go...* the whole point of balloons is to teach small children this.

⇥ *A Hat Full of Sky* ⇤

People's whole lives *do* pass in front of their eyes before they die. The process is called 'living'.

⊰⊱ *The Last Continent* ⊰⊱

No-one is finally dead until the ripples they cause in the world die away – until the clock he wound up winds down, until the wine she made has finished its ferment, until the crop they planted is harvested. The span of someone's life… is only the core of their actual existence.

⊁ Reaper Man ⊱

Inside every old person is a young person wondering what happened.

Moving Pictures

A man's not dead while his name is still spoken.

⊶ Going Postal ⊷

Why do you go away? So that you can come back. So that you can see the place you came from with new eyes and extra colours. And the people there see you differently, too. Coming back to where you started is not the same as never leaving.

⇥ A Hat Full of Sky ⇤

When in doubt, choose to live.

Thief of Time

So much universe, and so little time.

The Last Hero

There's times when you look at the universe and you think, 'What about me?' and you can just hear the universe replying, 'Well, what about you?'

+≡ *Thief of Time* ≡+

DON'T THINK OF IT AS DYING, said Death. JUST THINK OF IT AS LEAVING EARLY TO AVOID THE RUSH.

⊱ *Good Omens* ⊰

The universe is, instant by instant, recreated anew… there is in truth no past, only a memory of the past. Blink your eyes, and the world you see next did not exist when you closed them. Therefore… the only appropriate state of the mind is surprise. The only appropriate state of the heart is joy. The sky you see now, you have never seen before. The perfect moment is now. Be glad of it.

+≔ *Thief of Time* ≕+

ANIMALS

Pets are always a great help in times of stress.
And in times of starvation too.

⊷ Small Gods ⊷

Lots of people are animals inside. Lots of animals are people inside.

➤ Witches Abroad ➤

Dogs are not like cats, who amusingly tolerate humans only until someone comes up with a tin opener that can be operated with a paw. Men made dogs.

Men at Arms

Humans, eh? Think they're lords of creation.
Not like us cats. We *know* we are. Ever see a cat
feed a human? Case proven.

*The Amazing Maurice and His
Educated Rodents*

Animals never spend time dividing experience into little bits and speculating about all the bits they've missed. The whole panoply of the universe has been neatly expressed to them as things to (a) mate with, (b) eat, (c) run away from, and (d) rocks.

Equal Rites

Animals can't murder. Only us superior races can murder. That's one of the things that sets us apart from animals.

Lords and Ladies

RELIGION

I'd rather be a rising ape than a falling angel.

Guardian

Goodness is about what you do. Not what you pray to.

⊷ Snuff ⊶

There is a rumour going around that I have found God. I think this is unlikely because I have enough difficulty finding my keys, and there is empirical evidence that *they* exist.

⊷ 'The God Moment', *Mail on Sunday* ⊷

What have I always believed?

That on the whole, and by and large, if a man lived properly, not according to what any priests said, but according to what seemed decent and honest *inside*, then it would, at the end, more or less, turn out all right.

⇥ *Small Gods* ⇤

If you stopped tellin' people it's all sorted out after they're dead, they might try sorting it all out while they're alive.

Good Omens

Humans! They lived in a world where the grass continued to be green and the sun rose every day and flowers regularly turned into fruit, and what impressed them? Weeping statues. And wine made out of water! A mere quantum-mechanistic tunnel effect that'd happen anyway if you were prepared to wait zillions of years. As if the turning of sunlight into wine, by means of vines and grapes and time and enzymes, wasn't a thousand times more impressive and happened all the time...

Small Gods

'Atheism Is Also A Religious Position,' Dorfl rumbled.

'No it's not!' said Constable Visit. 'Atheism is a *denial* of a god.'

'Therefore It Is A Religious Position,' said Dorfl. 'Indeed, A True Atheist Thinks Of The Gods Constantly, Albeit In Terms of Denial. Therefore, Atheism Is A Form Of Belief. If The Atheist Truly Did Not Believe, He Or She Would Not Bother To Deny.'

＋═ *Feet of Clay* ═＋

He was determined to discover the underlying logic behind the universe.

Which was going to be hard, because there wasn't one.

 Mort

Some of the most terrible things in the world are done by people who think, genuinely think, that they're doing it for the best, especially if there is some god involved.

— Snuff —

The universe clearly operates for the benefit of humanity. This can be readily seen from the convenient way the sun comes up in the morning, when people are ready to start the day.

⊰ Hogfather ⊱

When you hit your thumb with an eight-pound hammer it's nice to be able to blaspheme. It takes a very special and strong-minded kind of atheist to jump up and down with their hand clasped under their other armpit and shout, 'Oh, random-fluctuations-in-the-space-time-continuum!' or 'Aaargh, primitive-and-outmoded-concept on a crutch!'

＝ *Men at Arms* ＝

POLITICS

You do need rules. Driving on the left (or the right or, in parts of Europe, on the left and the right as the mood takes you) is a rule which works, since following it means you're more likely to reach your intended rather than your final destination.

⤚ alt.fan.pratchett ⤛

Taxation is just a sophisticated way of demanding money with menaces.

≫ Night Watch ≪

Don't put your trust in revolutions. They always come around again. That's why they're called revolutions.

→ Night Watch ←

Fear is strange soil. Mainly it grows obedience like corn, which grows in rows and makes weeding easy. But sometimes it grows the potatoes of defiance, which flourish underground.

Small Gods

'The Ephebians believed that every man should have the vote (provided that he wasn't poor, foreign nor disqualified by reason of being mad, frivolous or a woman). Every five years someone was elected to be Tyrant, provided he could prove that he was honest, intelligent, sensible and trustworthy. Immediately after he was elected, of course, it was obvious to everyone that he was a criminal madman and totally out of touch with the view of the ordinary philosopher in the street looking for a towel. And then five years later they elected another one just like him, and really it was amazing how intelligent people kept on making the same mistakes.

+═ *Small Gods* ═+

What kind of man would put a known criminal in charge of a major branch of government? Apart from, say, the average voter.

Going Postal

'I'm sure we can pull together, sir.'

Lord Vetinari raised his eyebrows. 'Oh, I do hope not, I really do hope not. Pulling together is the aim of despotism and tyranny. Free men pull in all kinds of directions.'

+= *The Truth* =+

You can't go around building a better world for people. Only people can build a better world for people. Otherwise it's just a cage.

≒ Witches Abroad ≓

Two types of people laugh at the law: those that break it and those that make it.

⊶ Night Watch ⊷

Vimes didn't like the phrase 'The innocent have nothing to fear,' believing the innocent had everything to fear, mostly from the guilty but in the longer term even more from those who say things like 'The innocent have nothing to fear.'

 Snuff

A lot hinges on the fact that, in most circumstances, people are not allowed to hit you with a mallet. They put up all kinds of visible and invisible signs that say 'Do not do this' in the hope that it'll work, but if it doesn't, then they shrug, because there is, really, no real mallet at all.

+≫ *Unseen Academicals* ≪+

It is a long-cherished tradition among a certain type of military thinker that huge casualties are the main thing. If they are on the other side then this is a valuable bonus.

Jingo

WORDS
& WRITING

The pen is mightier than the sword… if the sword is very small and the pen is very sharp.

⊷ The Light Fantastic ⊶

People think that stories are shaped by people.
In fact, it's the other way around.

— Witches Abroad —

The reason that clichés become clichés is that they are the hammers and screwdrivers in the toolbox of communication.

Guards! Guards!

Words are the litmus paper of the mind. If you find yourself in the power of someone who will use the word 'commence' in cold blood, go somewhere else very quickly.

━ *Small Gods* ━

A good bookshop is just a genteel Black Hole that knows how to read.

⊷ Guards! Guards! ⊶

Stories of imagination tend to upset those without one.

⇥ Introduction to *The Ultimate Encyclopedia of Fantasy* ⇤

It is true that words have power, and one of the things they are able to do is get out of someone's mouth before the speaker has the chance to stop them.

+≡ *Wyrd Sisters* ≡+

William wondered why he always disliked people who said 'no offence meant'. Maybe it was because they found it easier to say 'no offence meant' than actually refrain from giving offence.

+≈ *The Truth* ≈+

Five exclamation marks, the sure sign of an insane mind.

⊷ Reaper Man ⊶

People like to be told what they already know. Remember that. They get uncomfortable when you tell them *new* things. New things . . . well, new things aren't what they expect. They like to know that, say, a dog will bite a man. That is what dogs do. They don't want to know that a man bites a dog, because the world is not supposed to happen like that.

In short, what people *think* they want is news, but what they really crave is *olds*.

The Truth

If you don't turn your life into a story, you just become a part of someone *else*'s story.

⊸⊷ *The Amazing Maurice and His Educated Rodents* ⊷⊶

BY TERRY PRATCHETT

THE DISCWORLD® SERIES

The Colour of Magic
The Light Fantastic
Equal Rites
Mort
Sourcery
Wyrd Sisters
Pyramids
Guards! Guards!
Eric (illustrated by Josh Kirby)
Moving Pictures
Reaper Man
Witches Abroad
Small Gods
Lords and Ladies
Men at Arms
Soul Music
Interesting Times
Maskerade

Feet of Clay
Hogfather
Jingo
The Last Continent
Carpe Jugulum
The Fifth Elephant
The Truth
Thief of Time
The Last Hero (illustrated by Paul Kidby)
The Amazing Maurice and His Educated Rodents
(for young adults)
Night Watch
The Wee Free Men (for young adults)
Monstrous Regiment
A Hat Full of Sky (for young adults)
Going Postal
Thud!
Wintersmith (for young adults)
Making Money
Unseen Academicals
I Shall Wear Midnight (for young adults)
Snuff
Raising Steam
The Shepherd's Crown (for young adults)

NON-DISCWORLD BOOKS
The Dark Side of the Sun
Strata
The Unadulterated Cat (illustrated by Gray Jolliffe)
Good Omens (with Neil Gaiman)

SHORTER WRITING
A Blink of the Screen
A Slip of the Keyboard

WITH STEPHEN BAXTER
The Long Earth
The Long War
The Long Mars
The Long Utopia
The Long Cosmos

NON-DISCWORLD BOOKS FOR YOUNG ADULTS
The Carpet People
Truckers
Diggers
Wings
Only You Can Save Mankind

Johnny and the Dead
Johnny and the Bomb
Nation
Dodger
Dragons at Crumbling Castle

A complete list of Terry Pratchett ebooks and audio books as well as other books based on the Discworld series – illustrated screenplays, graphic novels, comics and plays – can be found on www.terrypratchett.co.uk

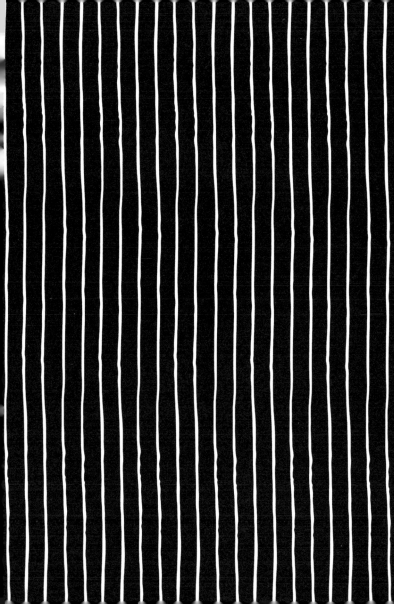